BET
YOU CAN'T

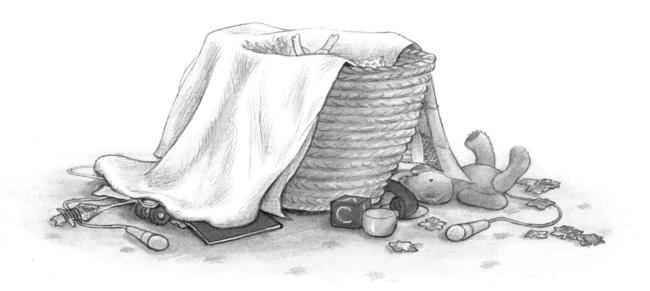

WRITTEN AND ILLUSTRATED BY

Penny Dale

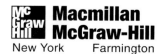
Macmillan
McGraw-Hill
New York   Farmington

D1122905

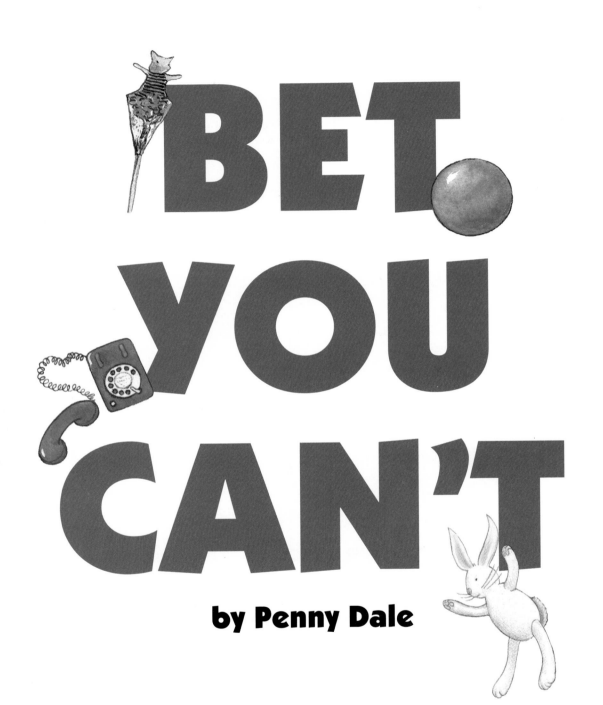

BET YOU CAN'T

by Penny Dale

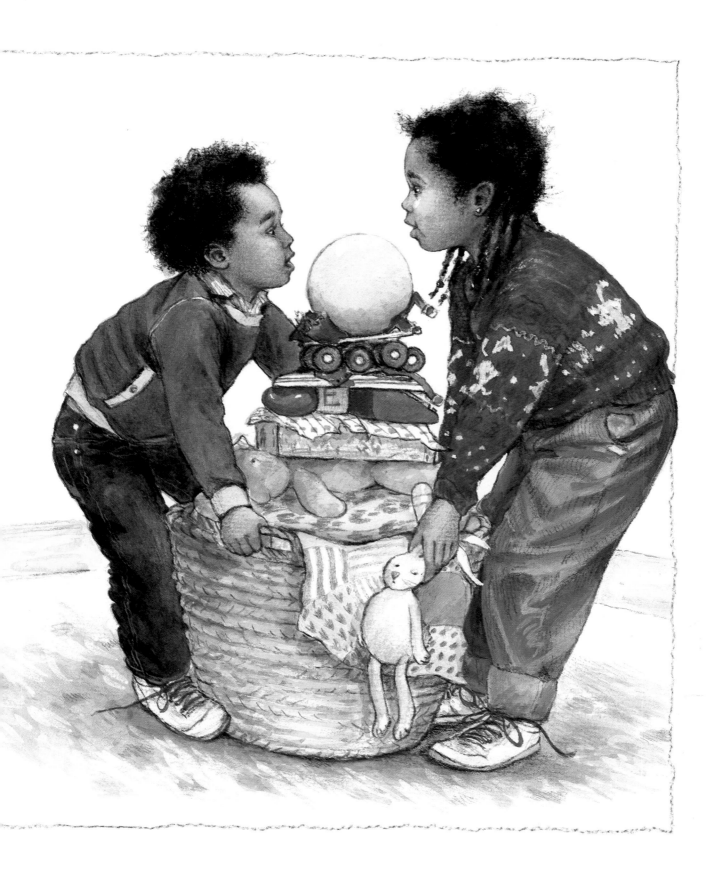

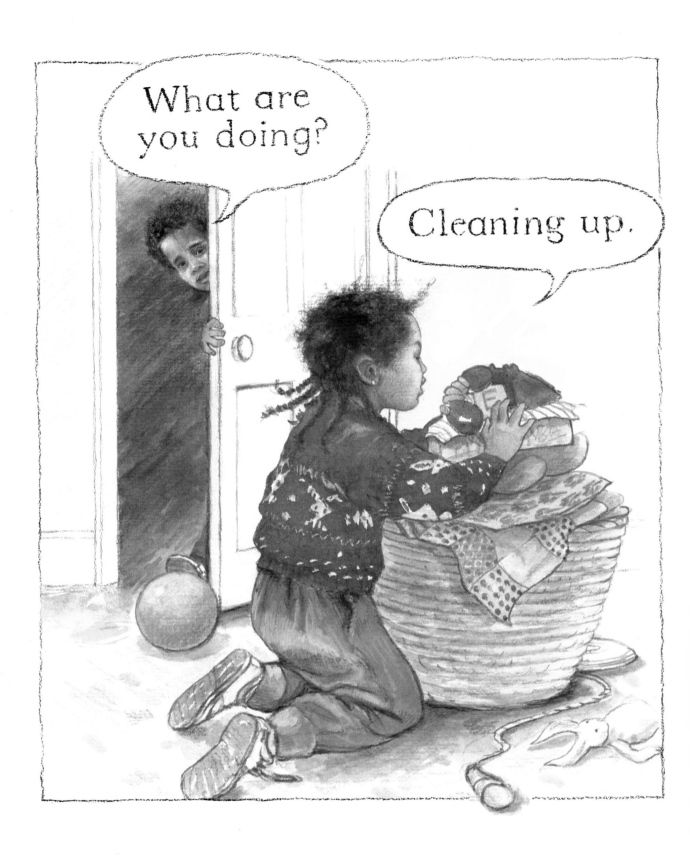

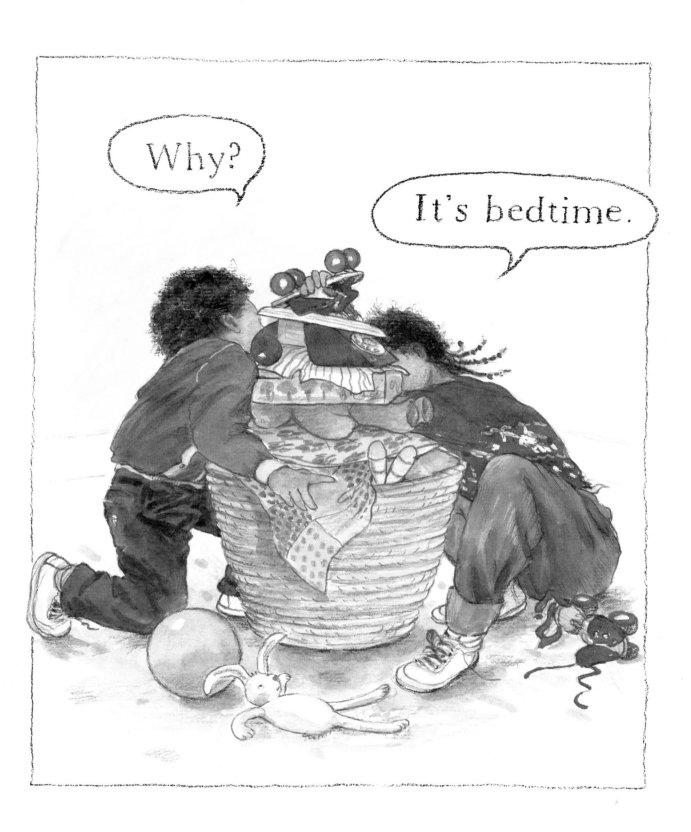

5

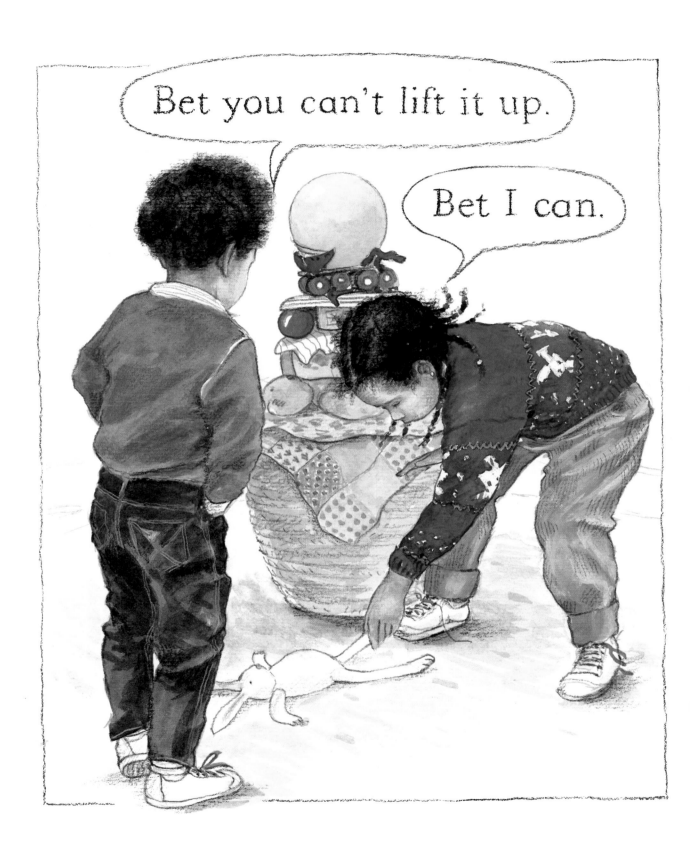

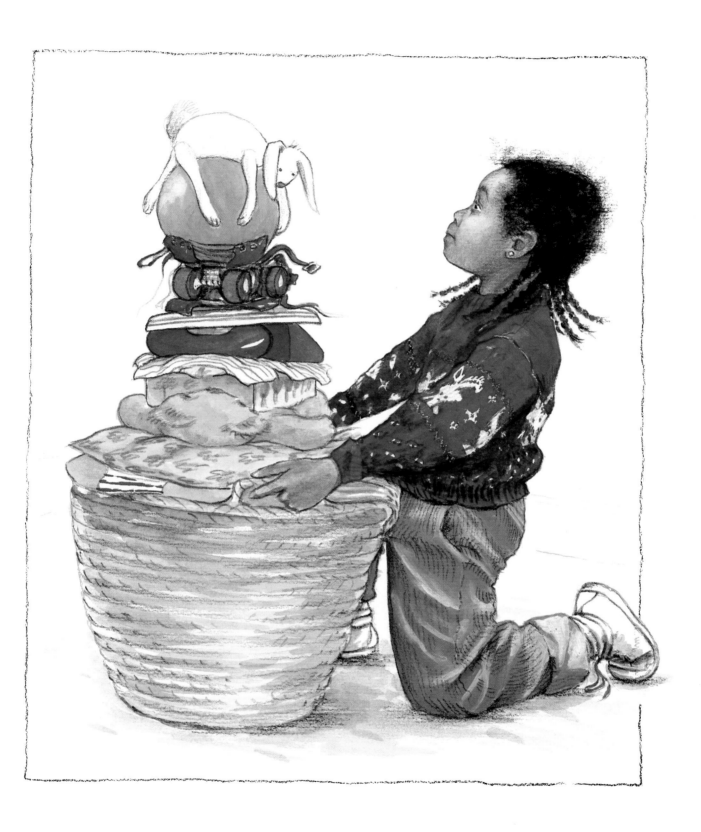

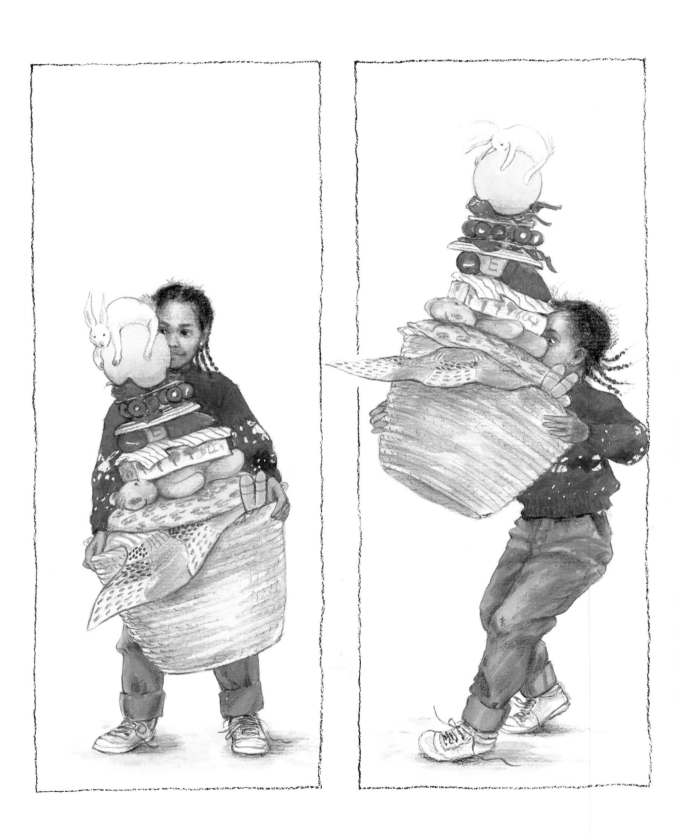

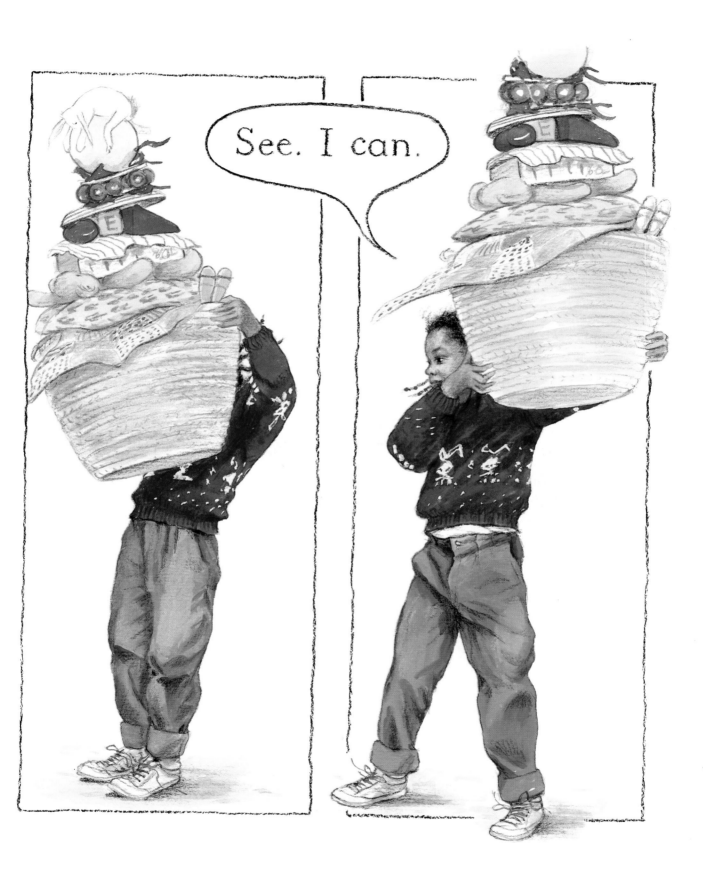

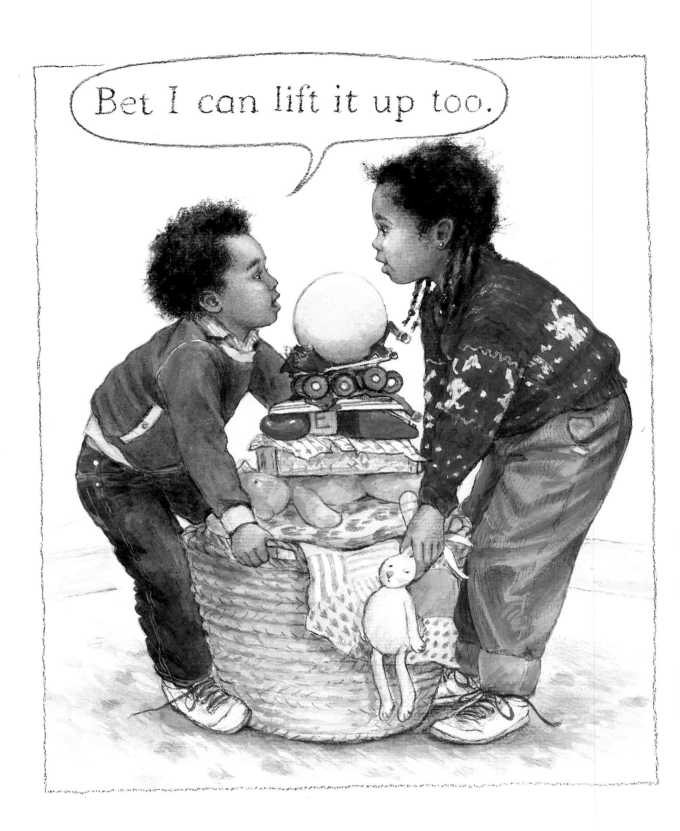

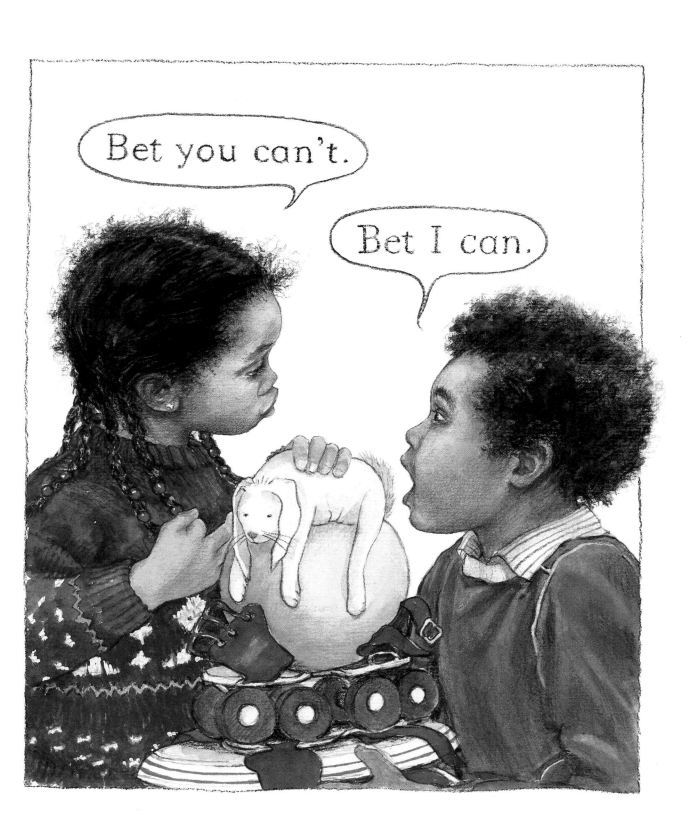

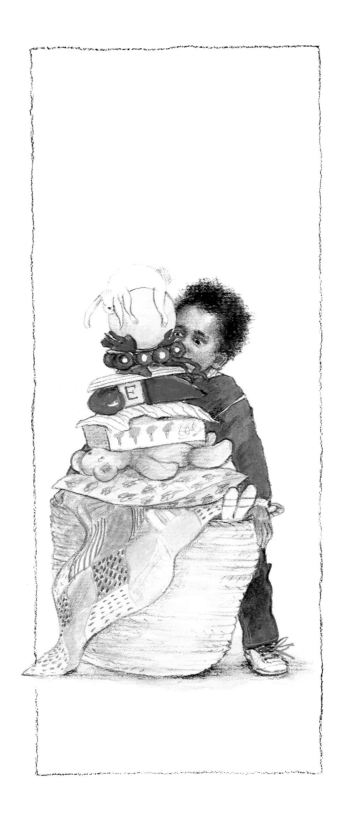
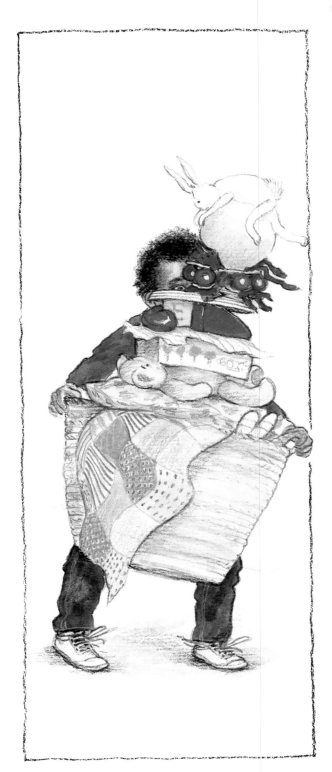

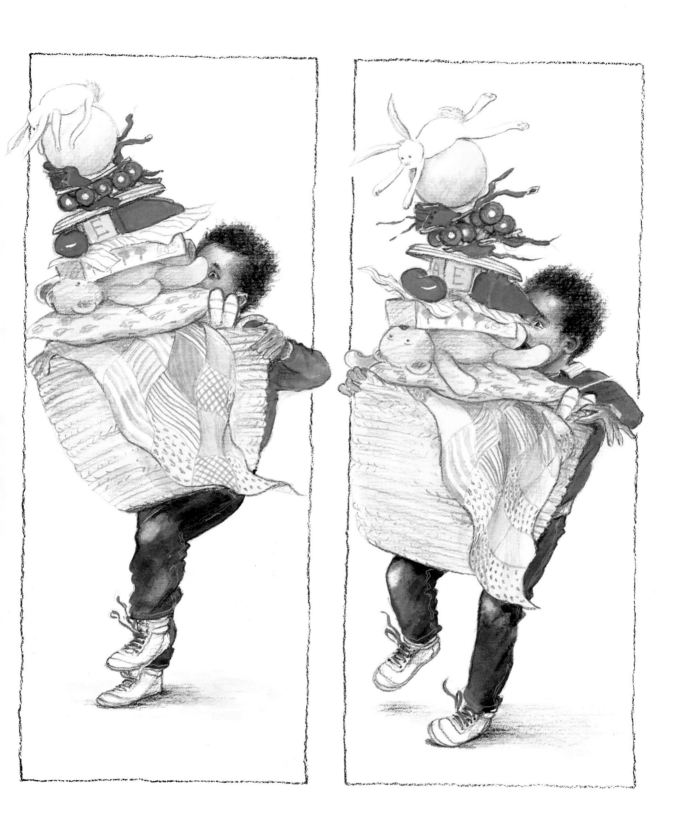

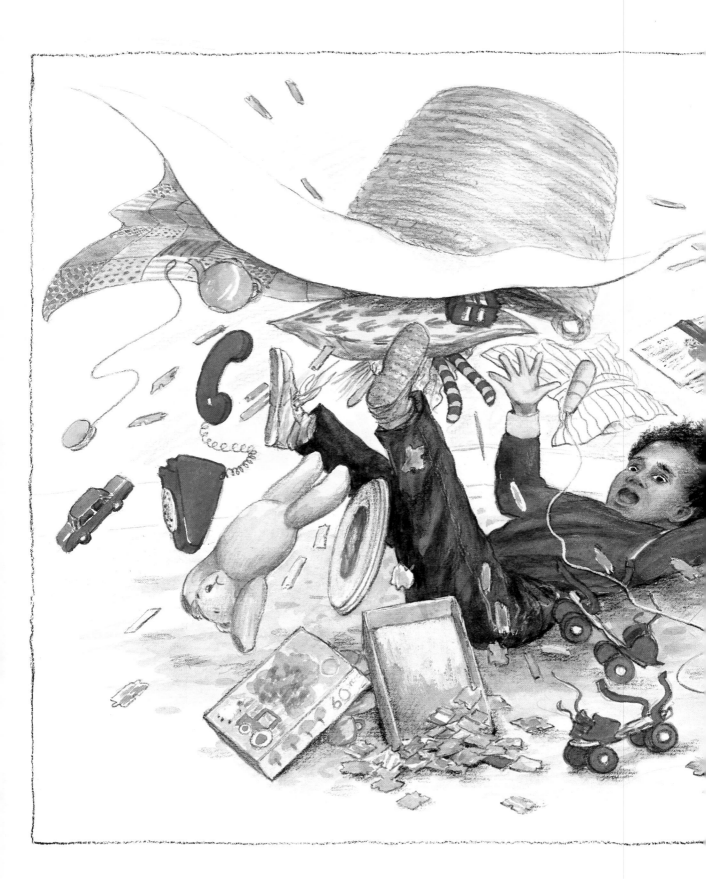

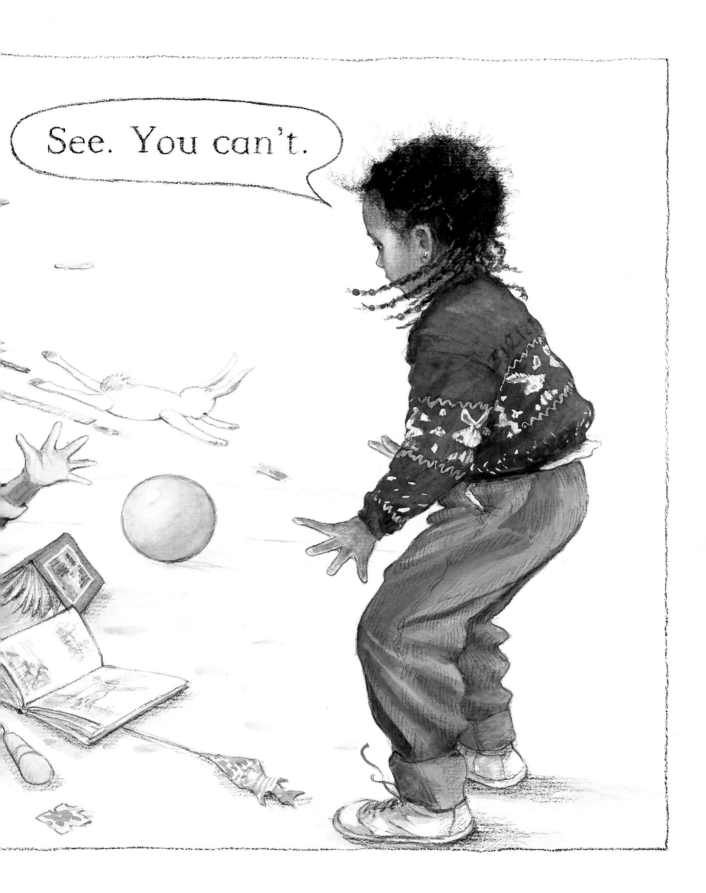

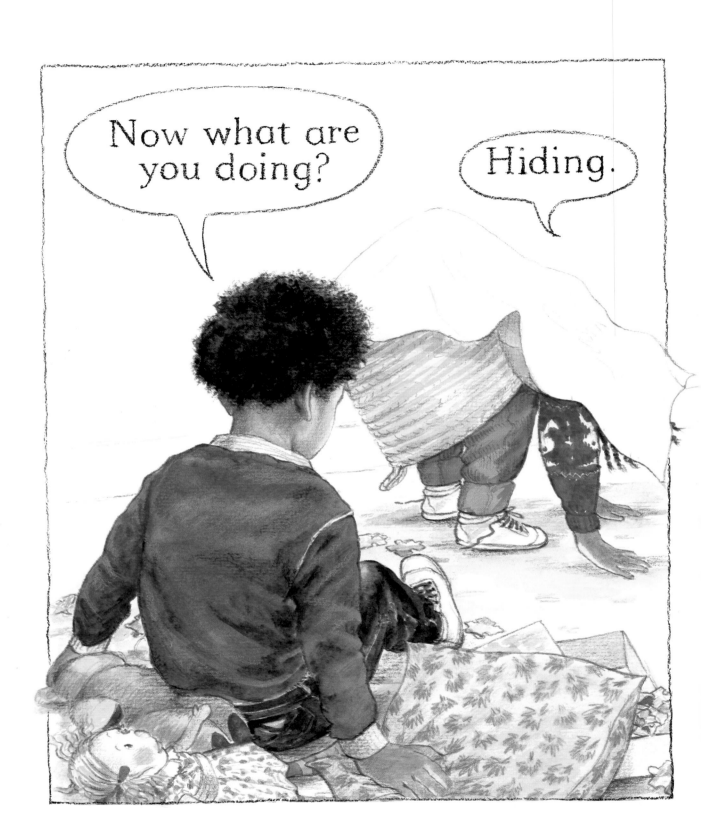

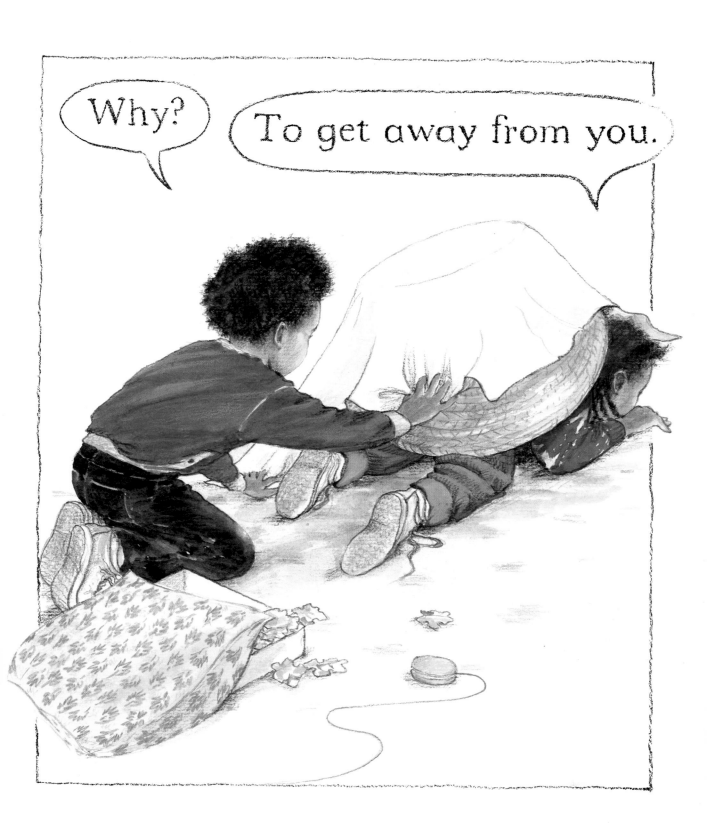

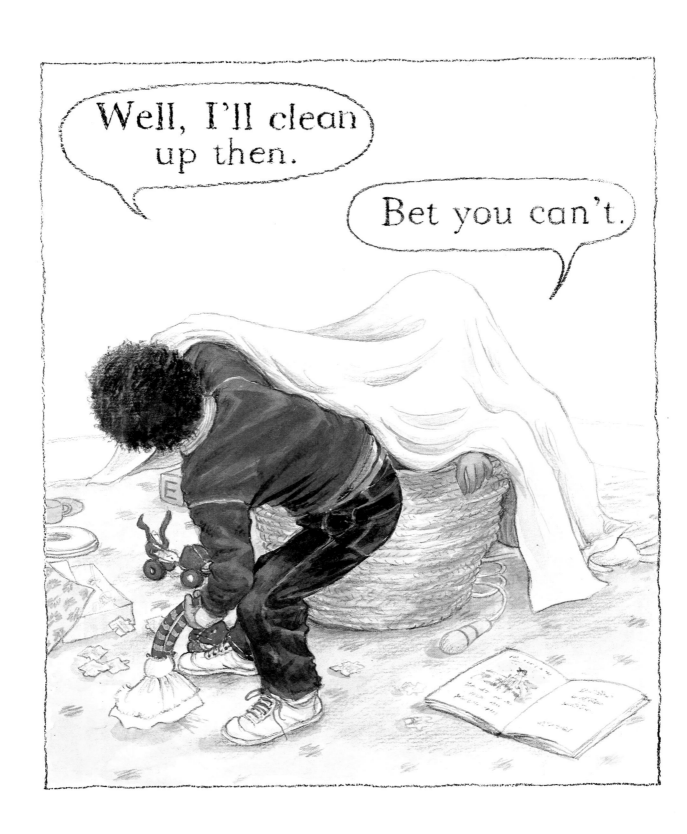

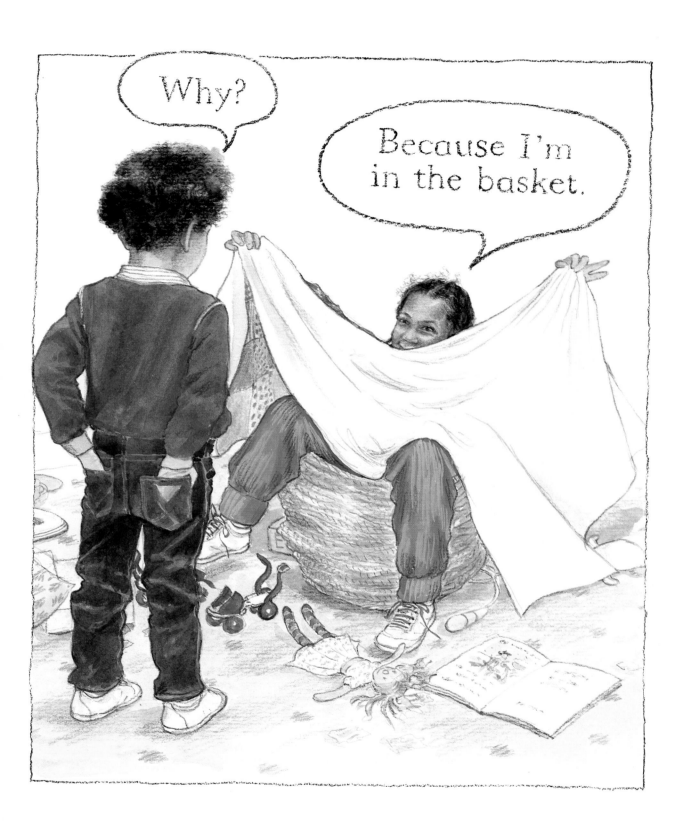

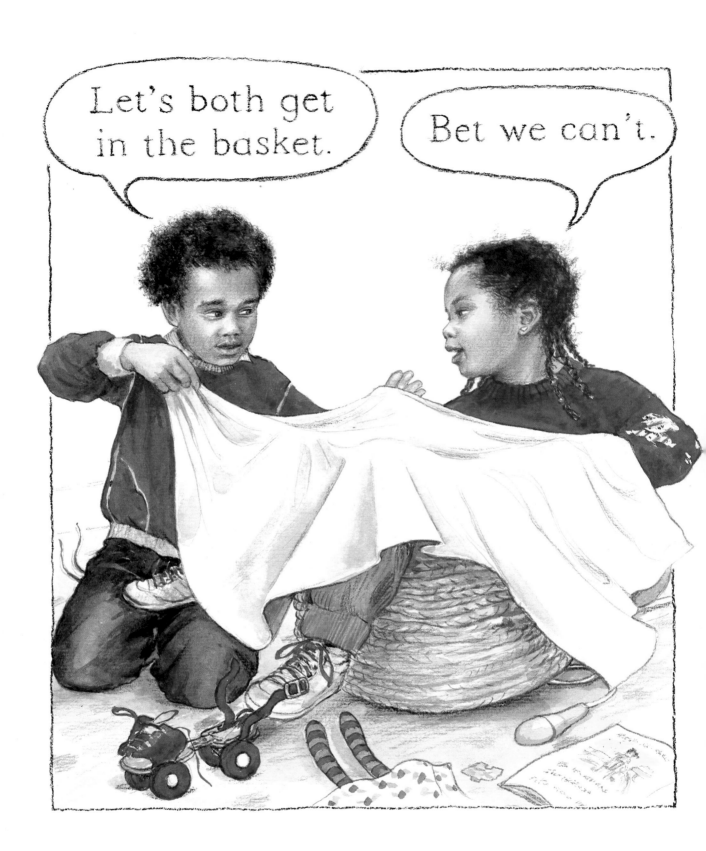

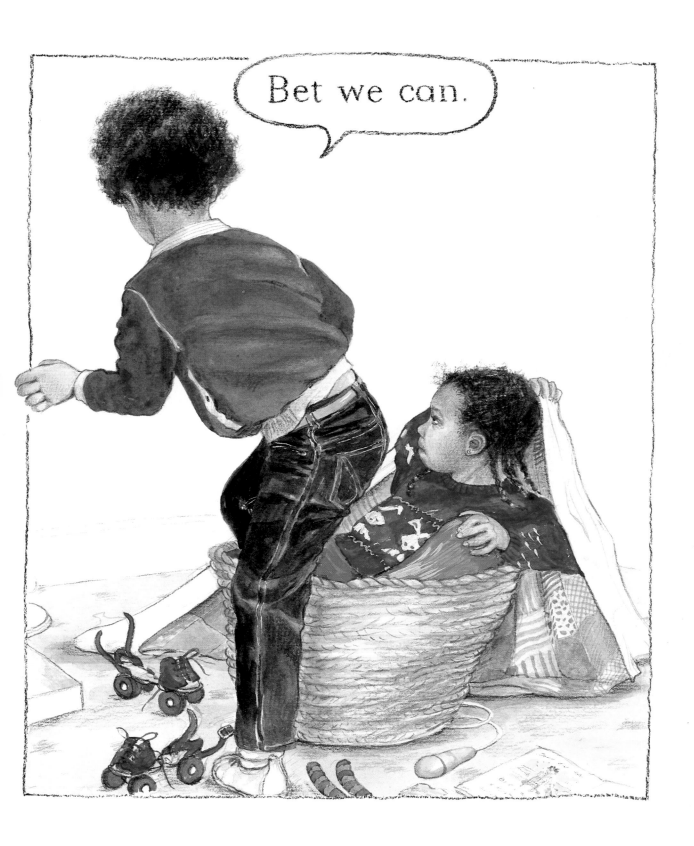

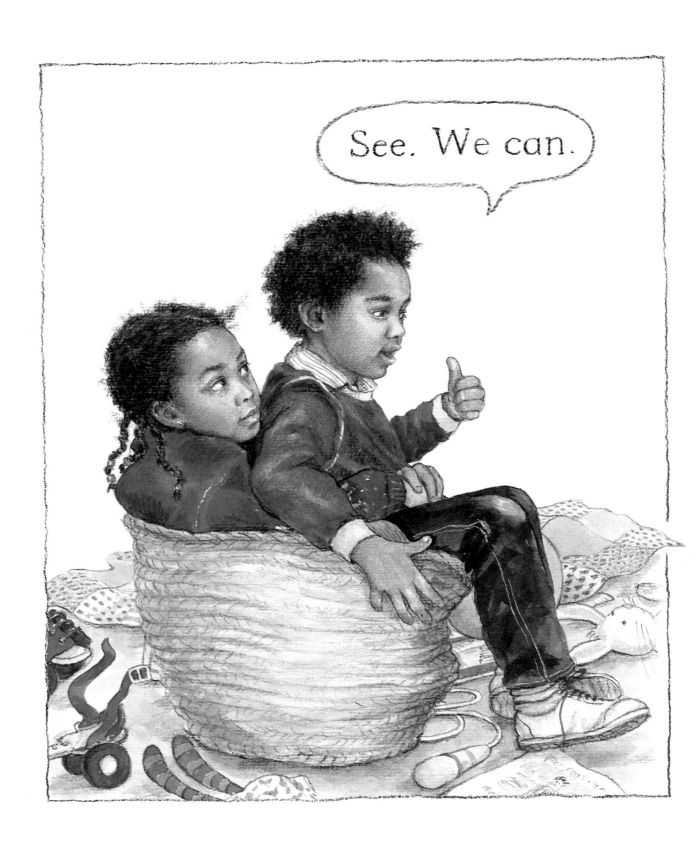

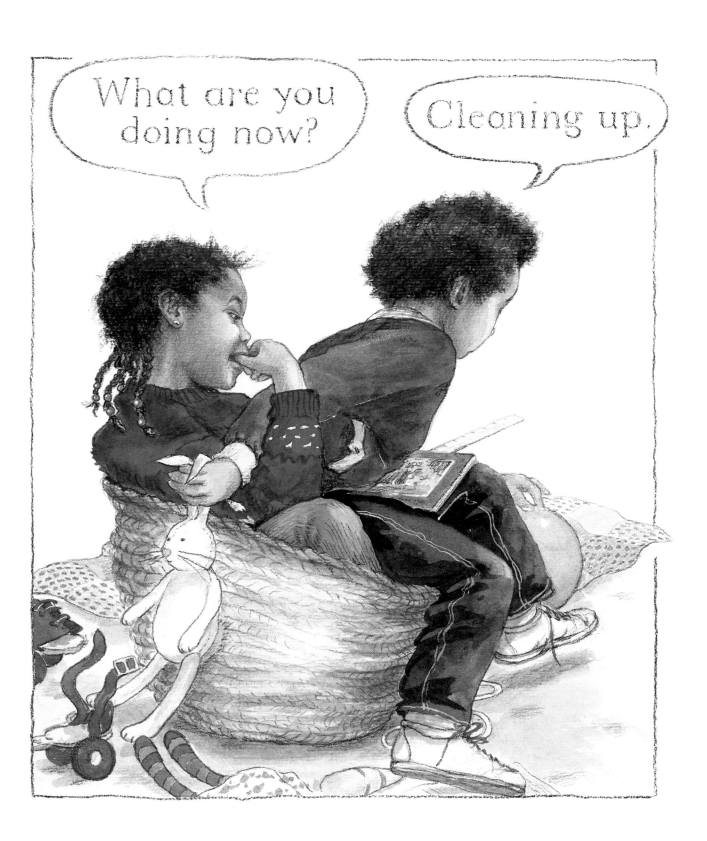

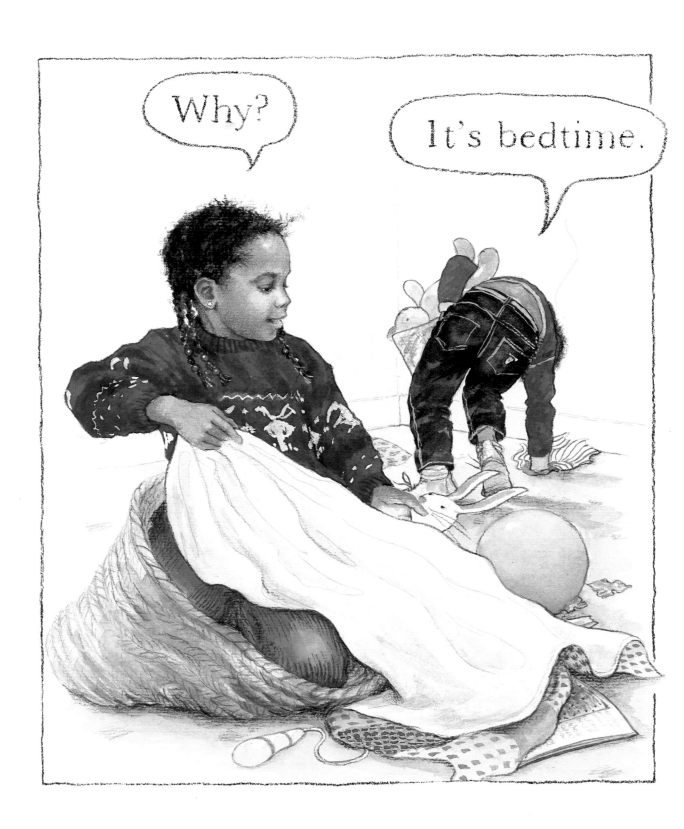

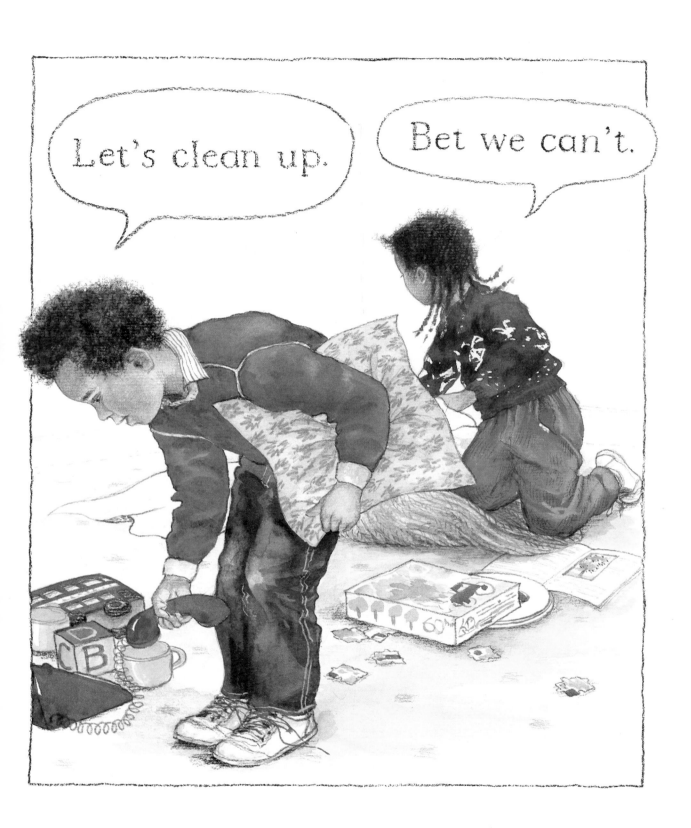

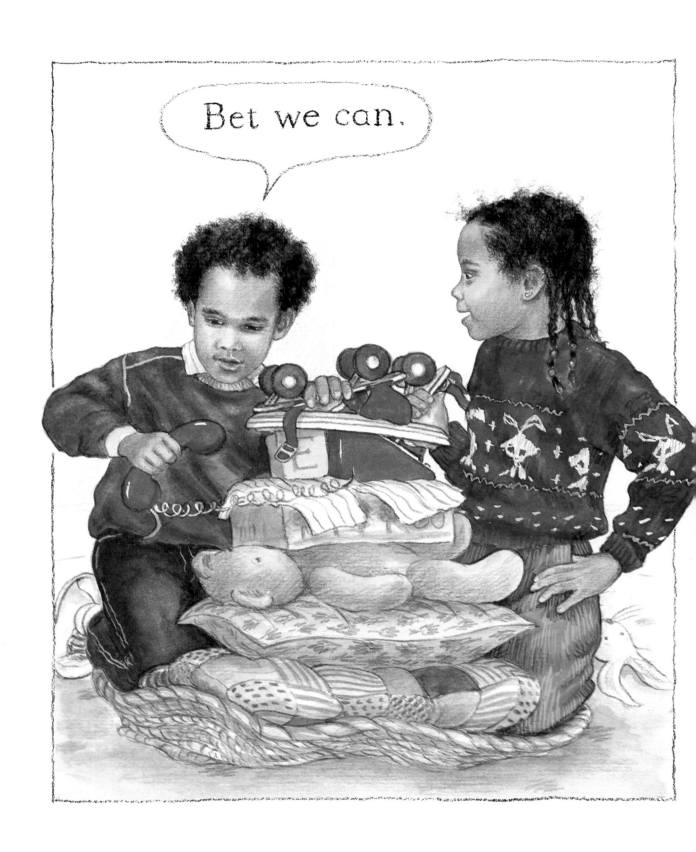

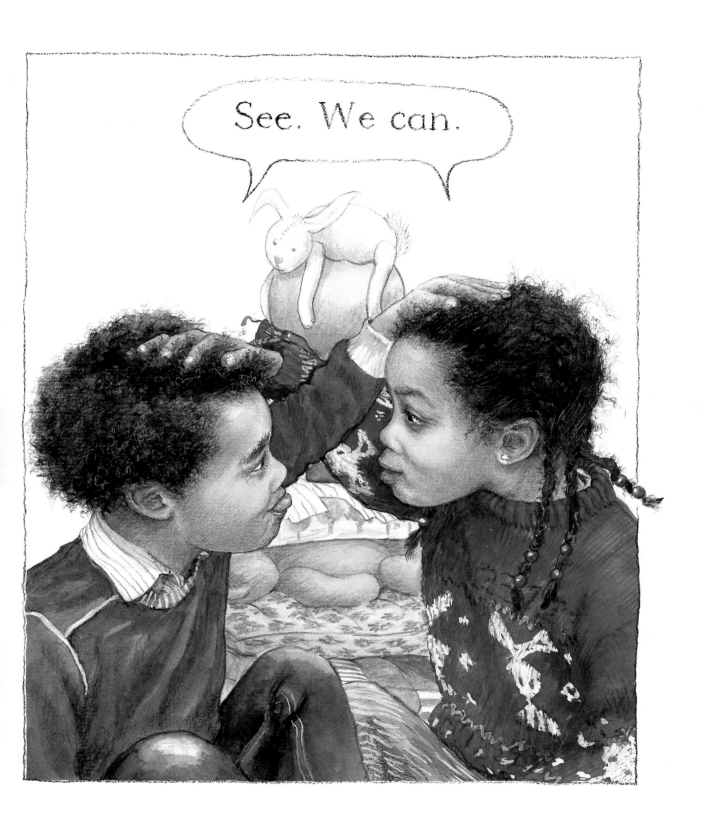

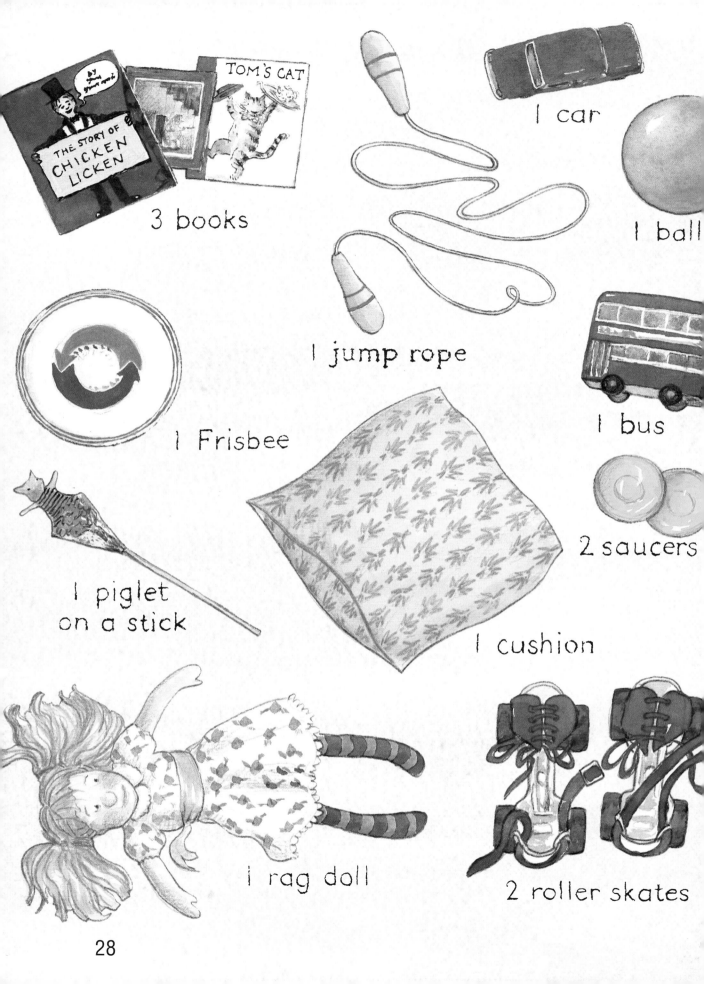

3 books

1 car

1 ball

1 jump rope

1 Frisbee

1 bus

2 saucers

1 piglet
on a stick

1 cushion

1 rag doll

2 roller skates

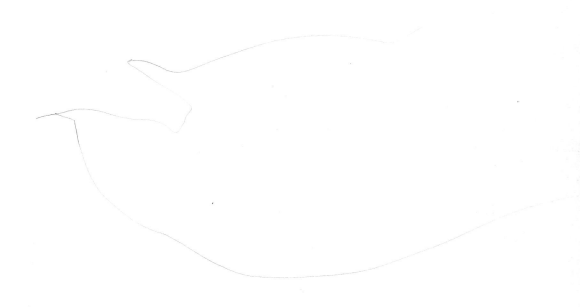